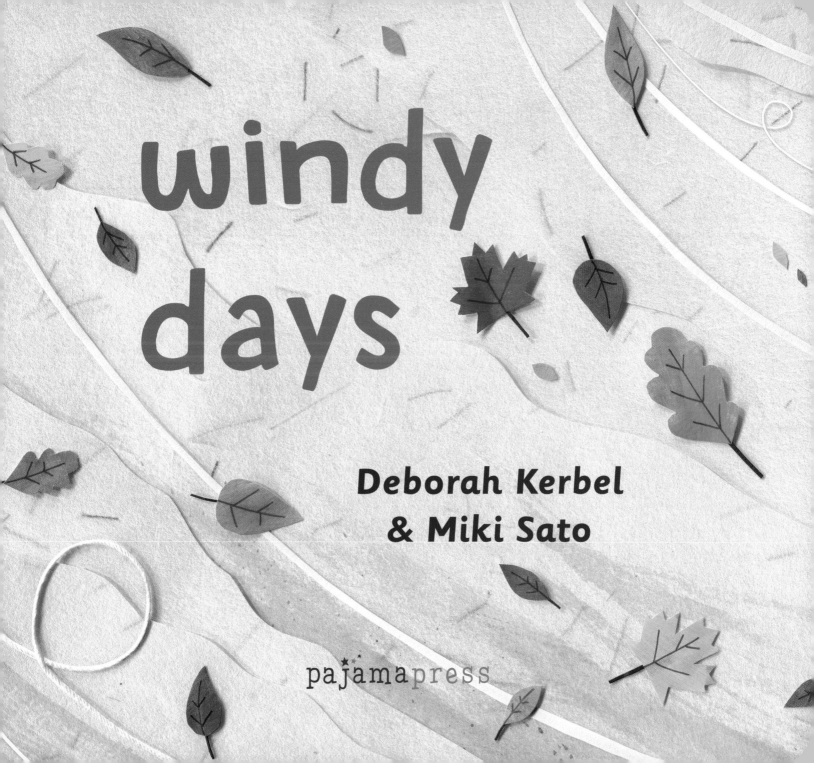

windy days

**Deborah Kerbel
& Miki Sato**

pajamapress

First published in Canada and the United States in 2021

Text copyright © 2021 Deborah Kerbel
Illustration copyright © 2021 Miki Sato

This edition copyright © 2021 Pajama Press Inc.

This is a first edition.

10 9 8 7 6 5 4 3 2 1

 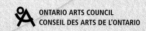

The publisher gratefully acknowledges the support of the Canada Council for the Arts and the Ontario Arts Council for its publishing program. We acknowledge the financial support of the Government of Canada through the Canada Book Fund (CBF) for our publishing activities.

Library and Archives Canada Cataloguing in Publication
Title: Windy days / Deborah Kerbel & Miki Sato.
Names: Kerbel, Deborah, author. | Sato, Miki, 1987- illustrator.
Description: First edition.
Identifiers: Canadiana 20210153830 | ISBN 9781772782172 (hardcover)
Subjects: LCGFT: Stories in rhyme.
Classification: LCC PS8621.E75 W56 2021 | DDC jC813/.6—dc23

Publisher Cataloging-in-Publication Data (U.S.)
Names: Kerbel, Deborah, author. | Sato, Miki, 1987-, illustrator.
Title: Windy Days / Deborah Kerbel & Miki Sato.
Description: Toronto, Ontario Canada : Pajama Press, 2021. | Summary: "Rhyming couplets celebrate windy weather, the sensory experience of wind, and the activities it makes possible from a preschooler's perspective. Mixed-media collage art shows young children engaging in outdoor activities, including scattering milkweed seeds, spinning pinwheels, flying kites, and struggling against a strong wind. A final page includes age-appropriate STEM activities related to wind"— Provided by publisher.
Identifiers: ISBN 978-1-77278-217-2 (hardback)
Subjects: LCSH: Winds – Juvenile fiction. | Kites -- Juvenile fiction. | Outdoor games -- Juvenile fiction. | Stories in rhyme. | BISAC: JUVENILE FICTION / Concepts / Seasons. | JUVENILE FICTION / Science & Nature / Weather. | JUVENILE FICTION / Sports & Recreation / Camping & Outdoor Activities.
Classification: LCC PZ7. K474Wi |DDC [E] – dc23

Cover and book design—Lorena González Guillén

Manufactured in China by WKT Company

Original art created with paper collage, textiles, and embroidery silk

Pajama Press Inc.
469 Richmond St. E, Toronto, ON M5A 1R1

Distributed in Canada by UTP Distribution
5201 Dufferin Street Toronto, Ontario Canada, M3H 5T8

Distributed in the U.S. by Ingram Publisher Services
1 Ingram Blvd. La Vergne, TN 37086, USA

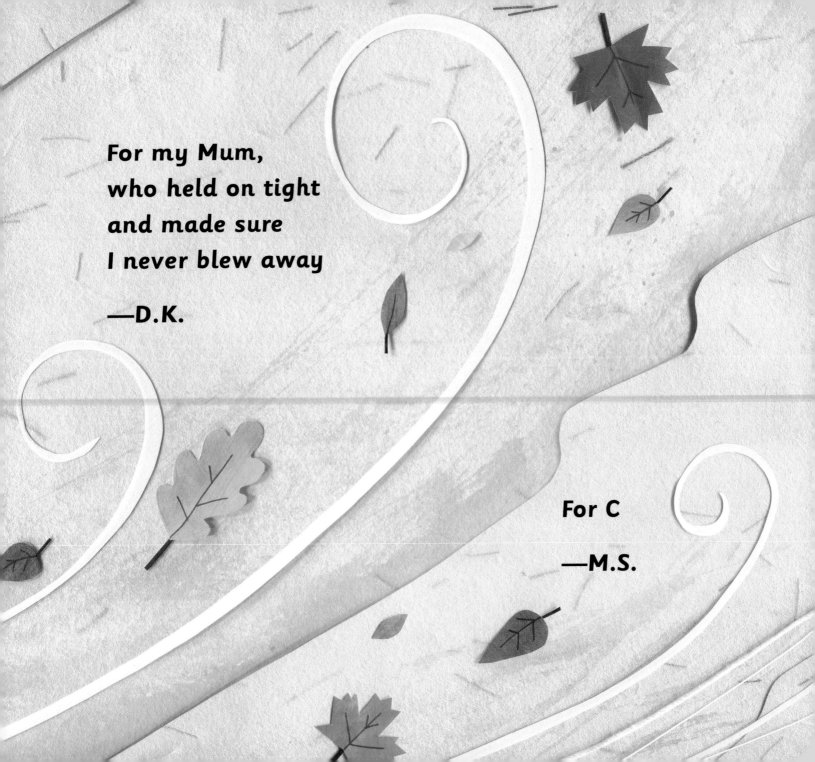

For my Mum,
who held on tight
and made sure
I never blew away

—D.K.

For C

—M.S.

Gentle wind, rising breeze
Scatters fluffy milkweed seeds

Gusting wind: whoosh and whirl
Flags a-flutter, pinwheels twirl

Whistling wind, stormy song
Tapping branches drum along

Autumn wind—geese take flight
Perfect day to fly a kite

Steady wind, turbine tower
Turning airflow into power

Swirling wind, swaying trees
Falling, spinning, dancing leaves

Sweeping wind blasts and blows
Tries to lift me off my toes

Roaring wind, howling sky
Restless storm clouds rolling by

Blustery wind burns and shrieks
Nibbles on my nose and cheeks

Icy wind, fading sun
A brand new season has begun

There is magic in wind...and science too!
Here are some fun experiments you can try yourself:

1. Take a pinwheel outside on a windy day. Turn it until you find the position that makes it spin the fastest.

2. Drop several small objects from waist height. How far will the wind carry a leaf? A twig? A pebble?

3. Lie down and watch the wind sculpt the clouds into new shapes.

4. Play hide-and-seek with the wind! Look for sheltered corners where the air remains still.

5. With adult help, fly a kite in a safe place away from overhead wires.

Big, puffy, low clouds are called **cumulus**.

Feathery far-away clouds are called **cirrus**.

Flat sheets of cloud are called **stratus**.

Can you find **cumulus**, **cirrus**, and **stratus** clouds in this book?